The Day the Fair Came
and other stories

This delightful collection of ten stories is just right for reading aloud at bed-time — or any other time of day!

There's a wealth of appealing characters, from Leprechaun George who can grant wishes to Cathie whose day at the fair ends in disaster.

Then there's the little girl who didn't like God; Andrew, who moves to a new house; Winston, who is adopted by a new mum and dad and baby sister; Jill, whose twin brother is always getting into trouble; and Ally and her brother Andy, who appear in two of the stories.

And there are two stories about kings. Read about what happens when the King plans to have a party. And how the people of Wishing-Down village prepare for a visit from the King.

The stories are especially suitable for the four to seven age-group. They are stories you will be asked to read over and over again!

THE DAY THE FAIR CAME

and other stories

Illustrations by Ray Mutimer

A LION PAPERBACK

Tring · Belleville · Sydney

This collection © 1984 Lion Publishing
All the stories are copyright and appear by permission of the authors

Published by
Lion Publishing plc
Icknield Way, Tring, Herts, England
ISBN 0 85648 724 4
Lion Publishing Corporation
10885 Textile Road, Belleville, Michigan, USA
ISBN 0 85648 724 4
Albatross Books
PO Box 320, Sutherland, NSW 2232, Australia
ISBN 0 86760 570 7

First edition 1984

All rights reserved

Illustrations by Ray Mutimer

Printed and bound in Great Britain by
Cox and Wyman, Reading

Contents

Introduction

The stories in this collection are all different. They have been written by different authors; they are about different characters and situations; they will appeal to different children at different times — but they all share something in common.

First of all, the stories have been chosen for enjoyment. The best-loved stories are read over and over again — and these have been chosen with that in mind. We hope these stories will give hours of pleasure to children — and to adults too!

And, just as important, the stories have been chosen for their content. They have been chosen because they have something good to say — about friendship, kindness, generosity, security, love and reassurance. But they are not at all 'goody-goody' — they are firmly set in the real world of natural fears, misunderstandings, disobedience and insecurity. Jesus himself used stories to help people understand his teaching and, in fact, *The King's Party* is based on one of his stories. *The Three Wishes* also takes Jesus' words 'It is more blessed to give than to receive' as its theme.

The Three Wishes

Colin Edmondson

Leprechaun George was a quick-witted, nimble little fellow, and you had to be sharp-eyed even to see him. But one day, Leprechaun George was not only seen, he was also trapped. It happened like this.

In a country, we don't know where, in a town, whose name doesn't matter, in a street, but not just any old street, there was a house. It was not a very big house, in fact it was a very small house and a very dirty house, and in it lived a lady by the name of Nothing.

'That's a very odd name,' you say, and it is. Mrs Nothing was named nothing, had nothing very much, and was expecting nothing, because, as she was always saying, 'Nothing ever happens to me.' Which was wrong, because on this particular day, something did.

On this particular day, Mrs Nothing was talking to her neighbour, which she did very often and very loudly.

'It's not fair, Mrs Drinkwater. I've nothing left, nothing at all. There is nothing in the pantry, nothing in my purse, and nothing in the bank. For breakfast I have had nothing at all, and I expect I shall have nothing for dinner or tea. And I have nothing to sell to buy anything either.'

Now, it so happened that Leprechaun George was walking by as she said this, and heard every word. This is not surprising, because everyone in that street, which was not just any old street, heard every word too. They heard it not only once, not only twice, not only three times, but twenty-three times, because Mrs Nothing told the same thing to everyone she met. She told Mrs Drinkwater next door, and the postman, and the milkman, and ever so many people. But if they ever asked what she would like more than anything in the world, she would say 'An orange. You see, I have never had an orange.'

Leprechaun George, however, had only heard it for the first time that day. Now Leprechaun George had met many people, some rich and some poor, but he had never met anyone with nothing. So he went to see her house for himself.

He slipped secretly through the front door. There was nothing. He went upstairs, there was nothing but dust. He went downstairs, there was nothing but cobwebs. He went into the cellar, there was nothing but dirt. He went into the tiny part of downstairs called the kitchen and there was nothing but bits. He looked into the pantry and squeezed inside to get a better look when — the door slammed, and, for the first time ever, there was something, or rather, somebody, in Mrs Nothing's pantry.

Mrs Nothing finished her talking all the way up and down the street and came in to enjoy, well . . . nothing. She opened the front door to see nothing. She went into the kitchen to put on nothing for dinner and opened the pantry door and, would you believe it, there sat Leprechaun George.

'Good day to you, ma'am', he said.

'Good gracious me!' exclaimed Mrs Nothing. 'There's *something* in the pantry!'

'It's only me,' explained Leprechaun George.

'Stop there!' shrieked Mrs Nothing, and slammed the door again just as Leprechaun George was about to get out.

Then Mrs Nothing sat down to think. You see, she had never had *anything* in the pantry before, and didn't quite know what to do now she had.

After half an hour, Leprechaun George knocked on the door. 'Are you still there, ma'am?'

'Why do you want to know?' Mrs Nothing was a little afraid of this question.

'Well, I just thought that if you'd have your three wishes I'd be on my way,' said Leprechaun George.

Mrs Nothing was delighted. 'Why — you must be a Leprechaun. Now I shall have something instead of nothing.'

Leprechaun George felt very sorry for the lady, but was getting just a little impatient.

'What's your first wish, then?' he asked.

'My first wish is to have thirty-six more wishes,' replied Mrs Nothing.

'Oh, very clever,' said Leprechaun George, 'but it won't do you any good.'

'Now, first of all I would like a nice orange,' she said, ignoring him. 'I think if I had an orange I would be happy for the rest of my life.'

But she wasn't.

Next she wanted eggs and bacon.

Then cream cakes.

Then a room full of money.

Then a new house.

Then . . . Oh, it went on and on.

Leprechaun George interrupted. 'Mrs Nothing, you've had nearly all your wishes . . .'

'Then I will have another seventy-two,' she answered.

Leprechaun George worked all day. And the next day, and the next.

'Mrs Nothing,' said Leprechaun George, 'have you had enough now? Can I go?'

'Oh no, not yet, not by a long way.'

'But you are the richest woman in the world and have more than anyone else. What else could you possibly want?'

'Happiness,' said Mrs Nothing.

'Well, if that is what you want,' said

Leprechaun George, 'give away everything until you have just enough left.'

So that is what Mrs Nothing did. She got her neighbour, Mrs Drinkwater, and all the people in the street she met, and everyone else she could find, and gave them anything they needed. At last she had given away so much that she found herself back in the little old house, in the street that is not just any old street.

'But I can't call myself Mrs Nothing any more,' she said to Mrs Drinkwater. 'I have so much. I have friends, I have happiness, I have time to help others and I have time to clean this dirty old house. And I have learned a lesson. It is not *things* that make life happy, but kindness and caring.'

'Good old Mrs Nothing!' said Leprechaun George, clapping his hands. 'You will have plenty of happiness now that you know that it is giving, not getting, that makes people happy.'

And Mrs Nothing laughed, and Mrs Drinkwater laughed, and all the street laughed, and that's why they call the street Friendship Avenue.

Then off skipped Leprechaun George, whistling happily.

'I hope they won't forget what Mrs Nothing learned,' said Leprechaun George to himself as he danced along.

And the people in Friendship Avenue never did.

The Little Girl
Who Didn't Like God

Armorel Kay Walling

Suzi was little. She liked little things. She liked cuddles and kittens, beetles and buttercups, small shiny pebbles, and just a *little* bit of cabbage at dinner.

But she didn't like God.

How do I know she didn't like God?

She said so. She said so one Sunday at dinner. It was Suzi's favourite dinner; only a *little* bit of cabbage, but lots of roast potatoes and gravy. Suzi stuck her fork in a roast potato and watched the steam come out and the gravy soak in. She thought 'Yum'. And she was just about to pop a bite into her mouth, when Dad said:

'First, let's say "thank you" to God, Suzi.'

Suzi scowled. 'Don't want to,' she said. 'Don't like God.'

Dad didn't ask why. He and Mum and Granny and big sister Sandra just bowed their heads and said 'thank you' to God for their food.

But Suzi didn't. She didn't like God.

(She ate up all the roast potatoes and gravy, though.)

Afterwards, Granny said, 'Anyone like a story?'

'Yes *please*,' said big sister Sandra.

'And me,' cried Suzi.

Granny opened a big book.

'Is that the book about God?' asked Suzi.

Granny nodded.

'Don't want it, then,' scowled Suzi. 'Don't like God.'

Granny didn't ask why. She just said, 'Come and have a little cuddle, then, while I read to Sandra.'

So Suzi climbed onto Granny's lap and had a cuddle while Granny read the story about how God made all the world. Sandra listened, but Suzi didn't. She didn't like God.

(She did enjoy the cuddle, though.)

Afterwards, she went into Granny's garden and found a secret hiding place under the lilac bush. It was only a *little* place — just big enough for Suzi to s-q-u-e-e-z-e into. It smelled lovely — and it was full of little things. First, she found a yellow buttercup growing in the grass. Then she found a brown beetle washing his face on a leaf. Then she found two shiny pebbles, just big enough for a fairy's crown. Tinker, her own tiny kitten, was in the secret place, too. He was asleep. Suzi stroked him. He opened one eye and began to purr, but he didn't run away.

Suzi forgot about God. She was too happy under the lilacs. She was too happy pretending she lived there — all alone with the little things. It was a good game and it lasted till supper.

And after supper, it was time for bed.

The sky was big and black now.

Suzi looked at the stars. 'How many are there?' she asked.

Granny smiled. '*I* don't know,' she said. 'I can't count them. *Nobody* can count them — except God. He made them. He put them in their places. He told them what to do. When we say our prayers, shall we thank God for the stars?'

Suzi scowled. 'No,' she said. 'I don't like God. *I hate him!*'

Then she stopped. She looked at the big black sky. God would surely be angry with her for saying that. Maybe he would throw something at her — a star, perhaps. She jumped into bed and disappeared under the covers.

She waited.

But nothing happened.

After a while, Granny put her head under the covers, too. 'Suzi,' she asked gently, '*Why* don't you like God?'

'Don't know,' said Suzi.

But she did.

How could she tell Granny, though? How could she explain that God was *too big*? How

17

could you like someone who was so big and bossy that he told stars what to do; who was so clever that he'd made the whole wide world; who was so important that you had to thank him for everything you ate; but who was so far away that you never ever saw him to find out if he was friendly?

Sandra bounced into the room. 'Can we have another story, Granny?'

'All right,' said Granny. 'Come and snuggle in with Suzi, though. I think she's frightened.'

So Sandra hopped into bed and snuggled down with Suzi, and Suzi came *very slowly* up from under the covers. She wanted to call out that if it was going to be another story about God, she wouldn't listen; but then she thought that God might be even more angry with her if she said that, so she didn't.

And thank goodness, it was only a story about a baby. Suzi liked babies; they were little, too. Suzi felt sorry for *this* baby. Hardly anyone wanted him. There was even a big, bad king who wanted to kill him as soon as he was born.

'Poor baby,' thought Suzi. '*I* would have wanted him. I would have given him a cuddle.' So she listened.

Granny went on with the story — about the little town where the baby grew up and about all sorts of kind and wonderful things he did when he *was* grown up. Suzi began to be suspicious.

She began to think that maybe this was another story about God after all — and she didn't like God. But she *did* like the baby — even when he grew up — so she went on listening.

And suddenly, there was Granny saying that God and the baby were somehow the same person and that it was so that *anybody* could be saved and go to heaven — even Suzi and Sandra and Granny — that the baby called Jesus had been born on earth and grown up and let himself be killed and come alive again for ever and ever.

Suzi thought about that. If *she* were the big bossy God who could tell stars what to do, would *she* have come down to earth as a little baby and let herself be hurt and killed, just to save people like Granny and Sandra? She wasn't sure — but she knew one thing: God must love Granny and Sandra ever so much to have done it. And as he'd done it for Suzi, too, then it must mean that the big bossy God loved her!

Suzi looked out at the starry sky and thought about big things. Then she remembered her secret place under the lilacs and thought about little things. She thought about everything she liked best; about cuddles and kittens, beetles and buttercups, small shiny pebbles, roast potatoes and gravy — and Granny. All given by God; all loved by God — even Suzi. *Now* she knew what God was like: he wanted to be friendly.

And she discovered something.
She liked God.

Winston's Important Weekend

Rachel Anderson

Two people looked after Winston. Aunty Pat was there all week, then Aunty Carol came on Saturdays and Sundays.

'I think I like you best, Aunty Pat,' said Winston. 'Aunty Carol looks cross.'

Sometimes Winston wished he had Aunty Pat all to himself, and didn't have to share her with the others.

One weekend, Aunty Pat didn't come. A new Aunty came instead. Winston crawled under the table and stayed there.

'Well, I don't care about Aunties either,' said Carmen. 'I've got a real mum and dad now. They're all my own. I'm going to live with them for ever and ever, till I'm grown up.'

Aunty Carol packed Carmen's clothes and her doll and Carmen went away with the mum and dad she said were all her own now. She looked pleased with herself.

Winston wished he could get a mum and dad

too. He asked Aunty Carol. She said,

'We'll have to ask your social worker next time she comes.'

Winston's social worker brought a photograph of a man and a woman. They didn't look as nice as Carmen's new mum and dad. The mum was holding a baby in her arms.

'They would very much like to be your parents,' said the social worker.

Aunty Carol pinned the photograph up in the dayroom and everybody looked at it. The mum and dad came to visit Winston. He ran and hid behind the dryer in the laundry. The mum found him.

'We've been looking for a lovely big boy just like you.'

'You don't want me!' shouted Winston. 'You've got a baby in your car already.'

'But we need you too, to be big brother for the baby,' said the mum.

Winston didn't want to leave, but Aunty Carol said, 'You'll come back and see us very soon.'

Winston sat in the back of the car with the baby. She held his finger and gurgled. They drove for a long time.

The mum and dad's house was much smaller than the children's home. But it had some nice toys in a cupboard. There was a photograph of Winston already in the kitchen.

'I like that,' said Winston.

'We've been waiting for you for a long time,' said the dad.

Winston didn't like the supper.

'Aunty Carol knows I don't like carrots!' he said, and threw his plate on the floor, and then crawled under the table. He wondered if the mum would send him away.

The mum cuddled him and read him a story. The dad went out to dig the garden. Winston went to help. That was fun.

Upstairs, there was a little shelf by Winston's new bed.

'To put your things on,' said the new mum.

'I haven't got any things,' said Winston.

'Then we'll find you some.'

They went round the house together and the mum found a fir-cone, three picture books, a postcard of a train and some marigolds in a mug. They arranged them on the shelf.

'Can I keep them?'

'Of course.'

Winston was in the room all by himself. It was very lonely.

'I'll leave the door open so you can see the light on the landing,' said the mum.

In the morning, Winston looked at the baby asleep in her room, and he looked at the mum and dad asleep together in the same bed. The dad opened his eyes.

'Would you like to come in and have another cuddle?' he said.

So they were all in bed together, and the baby had her bottle.

'I think I might stay always,' said Winston.

Winston, and his new mum and dad, and his new sister drove to the children's home to fetch Winston's anorak and his boots.

Ally and the Beautiful Balloon

Thelma Sangster

Ally was going to Lindy's birthday party. She was very excited because she had never before been invited to a party by any of her friends from play-school.

The invitation card stood on the mantelpiece in the living-room. 'Please come to my party on Friday, at three o'clock,' it said.

Mum made Ally a pretty dress to wear to the party. It was pink. Ally tried it on every day.

But on Friday morning Ally woke up feeling hot and achy.

Mum put a cool hand on her forehead. 'You don't look well,' she said, and rang for the doctor.

The doctor came with his black bag. He took out a listening tube, called a stethoscope. He listened to Ally's breathing and said, 'Uh-huh!'

Then he took out a glass stick, called a thermometer, and popped it under Ally's tongue, and held her wrist while he looked at his watch. Then he said, 'Hm-m-m!'

He looked down Ally's throat, and made her say 'Ah-h-h'.

Then he said, 'I'm afraid she's got a touch of flu. She'll have to stay in bed for a day or two.'

Poor Ally! All morning she lay in bed, feeling very ill. Mum brought her cold drinks to cool her down. She felt miserable.

By the afternoon Ally was feeling a little better. She wondered what was happening at the party at Lindy's house, which was in the same road.

'Mum, can Andy come and play with me?' she called. Andy was her little brother.

'Of course not,' said Mum. 'I don't want him to catch the flu as well. Now be a good girl and I'll bring you some jelly for your tea.'

Ally tried hard to lie still but she kept thinking about the party.

The wind rattled the window, as if calling her.

The children came home from school. Beckett Street echoed with their laughter.

Ally crawled out of bed and looked from the window. The children were skipping along. Their scarves streamed backwards in the wind. Their cheeks were rosy. They looked happy.

'I wish I could go to the party,' said Ally to herself.

She looked up at the wide, windy sky, at the clouds chasing each other over the house-tops, and she said, 'Our Father in heaven, please make me well so I can go to the party.' And then she

28

added politely, 'Amen'.

It was the very first prayer Ally had ever prayed by herself.

And something amazing happened.

Beckett Street was suddenly full of balloons.

There was a red one bobbing at the corner. A blue balloon sailed over a hedge and dropped behind a parked car. Floating along the opposite side of the road was a green balloon. And coming up the path to her front door as if pulled by a string was a white one, with red and yellow streaks.

'Mum!' called Ally excitedly. 'There's a balloon knocking at the door.'

Just then, down the road, came Lindy, Sara, Jenny, Gail, Tracey and Karen, all in their party dresses chasing the balloons. They danced, and laughed and waved up at Ally.

They caught all the balloons except the white one, with red and yellow streaks, at Ally's door. It was a beautiful balloon.

'Lindy sent you this balloon,' said Mum, bringing it in. 'It blew away from the party.'

And Ally lay quietly for the rest of the afternoon, gently bouncing her beautiful balloon.

That night, when Mum came to say goodnight, Ally had a special thank you prayer to say:

'Thank you, God, for my nice balloon. I wanted to go to the party, but you sent the party to me instead.'

And Ally went to sleep, dreaming about her beautiful balloon.

George and the Giant

Jenny Kendrick

Once upon a time, in a land far away, lived a huge and horrible giant, called Giant Gingerbeard. He lived in a dark, damp cave, deep in the forest, and every time children came near his den, he would let out a monstrous roar:

'ANYTHING BAD AND I'LL DO IT!'

Then he would hump and bump his huge feet out of the cave, and just as all terrible giants do, he would gobble the children up. He had dreadful manners too — he didn't even use his knife and fork!

Now, quite near to the Giant's forest was a small village called Wishing-Down village. Most of the people living there were quiet and peace-loving. They were kind people who liked to help. But one (his name was George) was not. Dear George! Some people in Wishing-Down village occasionally wished that George would wander too near to the Giant's den. You see, like most children, George knew how to make life difficult.

One long, hot summer's day in Wishing-Down village everything was just the same as usual — the shopkeepers keeping a wary eye out for

George and his tricks, and George's mum apologizing to everyone.

George was at his worst. He spilled the baker's flour; he hid the postman's bag; he pulled his sister's plaits; and, worst of all, he tripped up the greengrocer, so that fruit and vegetables and even the poor old greengrocer went rolling all over the place.

But then it was tea-time. People had left their work and gone home; the shops were shut, and even George was indoors, out of mischief. A quiet hush settled over the village and forest. Giant Gingerbeard, feeling rather tummy-full and tired after having all of Class Two for lunch (and a nibble of the teacher with his coffee), had given up roaring and shouting, and gone in to lie down and rest in the cool of his cave.

Suddenly the peace was shattered as a troop of soldiers galloped into the village square. Round and round they galloped, bringing astonished villagers to their doors and windows. Then the soldiers halted in the very centre, raised their trumpets to their lips and blew fanfares, till every person in the village had gathered round them.

The Colonel spoke. 'I bring a message from the King,' he said. 'In one week's time he will come to reward his true and loyal friends with medals. Be ready!' And with that, the horsemen turned and were gone, leaving the surprised villagers hardly able to believe their eyes and ears.

Away in the forest even Giant Gingerbeard had heard the noise and come to the mouth of his cave to listen. The Colonel's words came clearly over the quiet trees: 'In one week's time he will come . . . Be ready!'

As evening fell, the villagers could still be heard discussing the great news in the village square. One by one the villagers spoke, telling how they had decided to love and serve the King, by being kind to other people, and helping to look after his land.

'I'm the King's friend,' said Mr Peabody the butcher. 'I give extra meat to the poor and hungry, and I speak to them kindly, as though I am speaking to the King himself.'

'I love the King, too. I'm his friend, you know,' added Mrs Figge the draper. 'If someone comes to me in ragged clothes, I give them something new and nice to wear, fit for the King.'

'And me, I serve the King,' said Mrs Bellow. 'I treat strangers as I'd treat the King. I ask them in, and do my best to help.'

'I often see him at the hospital when I visit there,' said Mr Crane. 'We're good friends now.'

'I see him in the prison, too', said Mr Black. 'We go together sometimes. I love to help the King.'

'And me,' said George's mum. 'I like to help the King by helping travellers on their way. I ask them in to rest and offer them something to drink.'

Suddenly it seemed to George as if everyone except himself was a good friend of the King. He rushed home in a fright and hid himself in the dusty quiet underneath his bed. After all the excitement he was quite tired and soon his head began to nod. He rested his cheek on his arm and, half-asleep, he tried to think about the King coming.

The next moment he was fast asleep and in his dreams he saw himself waiting in front of the King for a medal. 'George,' said the King, 'Tell me how you have been kind and looked after my land.' George looked at his feet; he hadn't been kind at all. The King gazed down at him and George felt very uncomfortable. The King spoke gently, 'George, you have not tried to love and serve me. There is no medal for you, and no place for you here.' George turned slowly away and, all alone, set out to leave the kingdom.

'George, George!' George yawned and opened his eyes. 'What's the matter, George?' asked his mum, sitting down on the floor beside him. At first George just looked miserable, but eventually he asked, 'Mum, what will happen when the King comes next week?'

George's mum thought for a moment, and then she said, 'Well, the people will gather in the square and the King will look into each heart and read the story there. If he sees that you love and serve him, and help look after his land, he will pin a shining medal to your coat.'

There and then George decided that he would stop playing tricks, and start being kind. But he did wonder if the King would notice one week's kindness.

When mum had gone downstairs again, George got a pencil and some paper and his new rubber and, sticking his tongue out of the corner of his mouth, he began to write.

'Dear King,
I am sorry for my nasty tricks.
I will be kind now.
Your friend,
George.'

Carefully he put the letter into an envelope marked 'King, The Palace' and, making sure no one was looking, he crept off to the post-box.

Giant Gingerbeard had been trying to write a letter too. And, as Giants are never very clever, he was having a bit of difficulty. He knew that he did not deserve a medal; eating children is certainly not very kind at all. 'I'll have to leave my lovely dark, damp cave,' he mumbled to himself. 'The King will send me far away. And I'm sorry now. I'm sorry I've been so bad.'

The Giant chewed his pencil, and then he wrote:

'DEAR KING
I WON'T EAT CHILDREN ANY MORE.
PLEASE BE MY FRIEND.

GIANT GINGERBEARD.
P.S. I'M SORRY ABOUT CLASS TWO.
I'VE STILL GOT HALF THE TEACHER IF YOU
WANT HER BACK.'

Giant Gingerbeard licked the stamp — an enormous great lick — and squelched it on to the envelope. Then he sneaked out of his cave and, making sure no one was looking, made his way to the post-box.

He was just popping the letter in when who should come along but George. The Giant was taken by surprise and hissed, 'Don't tell!' before rushing away, leaving an even more surprised George to put his letter in the box.

That week everyone in Wishing-Down village noticed a change in George.

'George has been very good this week,' said the shopkeepers to each other. 'No tricks at all. Is he ill?'

'George has been very good this week,' said his mum. 'He hasn't played any tricks and he's even been quite helpful.' She *was* surprised.

And everyone in the village was talking about Giant Gingerbeard.

'What's happened to the Giant? Has he gone away?'

'He hasn't eaten anyone this week.'
'No, there are no children missing.'

'He's had fish and chips ten times this week!'

All week George worked very hard at being

good and every day he wondered if the King had got his letter. Tuesday, Wednesday and Thursday came and went. Everyone worked very hard cleaning and clearing up, and decorating the village square. On Friday George watered the flower-beds and polished the seats. Giant Gingerbeard swept his cave and tidied the forest.

And then the great day came. Giant Gingerbeard put on his very best clothes and gave his ginger beard an extra-special brushing. George had his best clothes on too. George's mum couldn't believe her eyes as George stood still while she tied his tie and smiled at her while she brushed his hair and washed his face *and* neck *and* ears! 'That must be the first proper wash you've had for months,' she muttered. 'Good job, too. The King will be here any minute.'

And then they were out in the street. What a noise and commotion! All the villagers, prinked and polished and dressed in their best, jostled and chattered their way into the village square. George stood shyly, holding on to his mum's hand. Someone else felt rather shy, too. Giant Gingerbeard was hiding round a corner just out of sight. Every now and then he peeped out to see what was happening.

Suddenly there was quiet in the square and then in the distance they heard the sound of trumpets and of marching feet.

'The King is coming. Hurrah!' shouted the

villagers. And soon the centre of the square was filled with soldiers, horsemen, bandsmen, guards, and at last . . . the King!

The King looked round at the cheering people then, raising his hand for silence, he spoke.

'My friends, you know I am here to give medals to all who love and serve me, who are kind and help look after my land. Come forward and let us begin.'

Then the King got down from his horse and one by one the people came. And to each coat, he pinned a shining medal. Last of all came George's mum and George.

'I got your letter, George,' said the King. 'And I can see that love and kindness are in your heart now. I'm so glad we can be friends.'

The King pinned one of the beautiful shining medals onto George's coat. George was almost bursting with pride and pleasure that the King had spoken to him.

Then the King looked round. There was one medal left. He picked it up and went over to where Giant Gingerbeard was hiding. The next time the Giant peeped out, he saw the King coming towards him.

'Ah, Giant Gingerbeard,' exclaimed the King. 'I've been wanting to meet you. Thank you for writing. I can see you have made up your mind to change your ways. Now everyone will know that we are friends.' And the King pinned the last medal onto the blushing Giant's coat.

The people cheered and shouted. 'Hurrah! Hurrah for the King! And George! And Giant Gingerbeard!'

Once more the King raised his hand for silence and then the village heard the very best news ever.

'I have decided to build my palace here,' announced the King, 'where every person is my friend. And every day we shall walk and talk together in the village square.'

And so it happened. A beautiful palace was built near Wishing-Down village and every day the happy King strolled in the village square with all his friends, and especially George and the Giant.

Moving Day

Wendy Green

'Andrew! Quick. Come and look. The removal van is here.'

Andrew came, but slowly. He didn't want the removal van to come. He didn't want all his toys and games packed away in boxes. He didn't want three huge men stomping backwards and forwards, loading everything into their big green van.

'You stand by the window and watch,' said his mother. 'And don't get in the way.'

Andrew watched. There was nothing else to do. The television was wrapped in an old blanket, his bicycle was trapped behind all the stuff piled in the garage, and Mum was so flustered it was best to keep out of range.

Even his mates had deserted him — Michael, Stephen, David. He'd seen them, rushing off to school, with no more than a quick wave in his direction. He kicked the skirting-board under the window angrily. So much for mates.

He was still sulking when Mum called the removal men for a cup of tea. They clustered awkwardly in the empty lounge.

'Cheer up, sonny,' said one of the men as he ladled great spoonfuls of sugar into his tea. 'It's not the end of the world.'

Andrew's scowl deepened. It felt like it. Everything familiar was disappearing, loaded on to their ugly great furniture van.

Even Mum was different. She would never stand there smiling if *he* tried to take six spoonfuls of sugar.

'Thought you'd be jumping up and down with excitement,' said the second man. 'Most youngsters are on moving day.'

'Think it's all a great adventure,' added the third. 'New school and all that.'

Andrew sidled out of the room without replying. What did they know about it? They hadn't met Miss Thomson, with her loud, booming voice. Even the top class trembled when she let rip. What if the teacher at the new school was worse?

'Do we have to move, Mum?' he asked, following her into the kitchen.

'You know the answer to that,' Mum said. 'Dad has another job. We have to live where the jobs are.'

Andrew stared unhappily round the kitchen. The cooker had gone, so had the washing-machine, and the refrigerator.

'You'll like the new house — once you get used to it,' Mum said in an encouraging tone. 'It's not that much different to this . . . only a bit more modern. Not so many nooks and crannies.'

'I like nooks and crannies,' Andrew said obstinately.

'I know,' sighed his mother. 'But you don't have to clean them. Come on. Here's Mrs Moore coming for the keys for the new people and I'm nowhere near ready.'

She bundled him out of the back door. 'You stay in the garden. I'm just going to do the final mop through, and I don't want you walking over my nice clean floors.'

'I should think not,' panted Mrs Moore. 'I won't delay you either, dear. Perhaps your hubby could drop the keys through the letter-box. I'm just going down the shops.'

She ruffled Andrew's hair. 'Enjoy your new home. Lucky lad. Wish I was moving house.'

'You wouldn't,' said Andrew's mother. 'Not when it comes to all the work.'

'No,' said Mrs Moore. 'You watch it, too. You know what they say. "New house, new baby".'

Andrew could still hear Mum laughing when Mrs Moore was trundling down the path.

A baby? Mum never said anything about a baby. They were no laughing matter. Michael's mum had one. It looked all right when it was asleep in the pram, but Michael said it didn't stay like that for long. It cried a lot, and was always hungry. And it leaked at the edges. He wasn't sure

that he wanted a baby, any more than he wanted to move house.

Everything was changing. It was all Dad's fault. If he hadn't got this stupid job . . .

'Stephen's dad goes to work in the car each day,' he said accusingly to Dad's back.

Dad eased a huge box of groceries into the boot of the car, and turned to look at him.

'Stephen's dad only works five miles away, and he has a flashy new car that isn't likely to fall to bits any day,' he said. 'Be a good boy and ask your mother if that's the lot. I think I saw your Snoopy rolling around somewhere.'

Snoopy was in the hall. So was his favourite poster. Mum had agreed there was no need to pack them until the last. Andrew carried them thoughtfully to the car.

He hugged Snoopy to him while they sat waiting for Mum to do the final check.

'That's it, then,' she said at last, settling beside Andrew on the back seat. She glanced at her watch. 'We're not doing too badly for time. We'll stop half-way and have fish and chips for dinner. Your favourite, Andrew.'

Andrew hunched in the corner of the car, and said nothing. He didn't really feel like fish and chips.

But after they had travelled for an hour or more Andrew's stomach began to tell a different story. Especially when they had to wait in a long queue at the chip shop.

'Can I have plenty of vinegar, please?' he asked when it was their turn. The man behind the counter scooped a huge pile of golden chips into a bag.

'I don't see why not,' he said, shaking extra vinegar on Andrew's portion, 'seeing as you asked nicely.'

Sitting in the car, eating chips from a newspaper, was great fun, even though it was moving day.

So was racing the removal van. It overtook them just as Andrew was finishing the last of his chips.

'They'll get there first,' he groaned.

'With that load on?' said Dad.' You must be joking. This old bone-shaker's still got some life left in her.'

But Dad would not overtake until he was sure it was safe.

'Hooray!' yelled Andrew, waving excitedly to the removal men when they eventually passed the big green van.

Dad tooted the horn. 'They'll never catch us now,' he said.

'Famous last words,' teased Mum. 'You know what usually happens when you say something like that.'

But for once the car behaved perfectly. Before long Dad announced they were nearly at the new house.

Andrew was out of the car and up the path as soon as the car stopped. He hopped impatiently on the doorstep while Mum fumbled with the new key. Inside the house he raced from room to room. It was bare and echoing.

'What are you going to put in here? Why is there a toilet downstairs?' he demanded. 'Where can I put Snoopy? Which is my room? Is it the yellow one?'

'One question at a time,' said Mum. 'You make my head reel. Whatever are we going to do with you?'

At that moment the doorbell rang.

'I bet it's the removal men,' shouted Andrew, racing to the door.

But it wasn't the removal men. A lady and a little girl were standing on the doorstep.

'Hello,' said the lady. 'We live opposite. Are you moving in today? Can we do anything? Would it be any help if your little boy came to our house to play while you get sorted out?'

'Yes, please,' said Mum. Before Andrew had chance to disagree he found himself bustled out of the house, and across the road.

'If you play in Joanne's room you'll be able to see across to your house,' Joanne's mother said, as she led the way upstairs. 'But don't make too much noise. You might wake the baby, and then you would regret it.'

'Why would we regret it?' Andrew asked, when they were lying on the floor making a fort from Lego.

'Because she's a pest,' Joanne said. 'She'd crawl straight through the middle and smash everything up.'

'We'd better have a quiet battle then,' Andrew said, selecting his soldiers.

Joanne nodded agreement. 'I can't make much noise,' she said. 'I've just been to the dentist and my jaw still feels funny where I had an injection.'

They were so quiet the baby slept until teatime, and Joanne's mother said she had almost forgotten there were any children in the house.

'That's not what our teacher says,' Joanne laughed. 'She says she could sometimes do with a pair of earplugs.'

'Does she shout?' Andrew asked fearfully. Noisy children were nothing to worry about. Noisy teachers were the problem.

'Only if somebody's really naughty,' Joanne said. 'But that's not very often. You'll like her. Everybody does. We do acting and all sorts. I wanted to go back after the dentist, but Mum said it wasn't worth it. I'm glad now. Our fort's great.'

Andrew was glad too. He had a new friend, and the promise of a nice teacher. Things were looking up. He could even face Joanne's baby, in spite of the mess she made eating her tea. She was quite amusing really, banging her spoon, and blowing bubbles with the milk every time Joanne's mother tried to give her another spoonful of cereal.

'We'll play tigers with her under the table when she's finished,' said Joanne. 'She likes that.'

So did Andrew. He was surprised to find it was dark outside when Mum came to collect him. The light was on in the new house and it looked warm and friendly.

Most of the rooms downstairs looked as if you could actually live in them now too. Apart from the kitchen. Dad had bits of television all over the table.

'The journey must have shaken something loose,' he said apologetically.

'Good,' said Mum. 'Then maybe we shall get a bit of peace for a change.'

'But there's football later,' Dad protested.

Mum glared at him. 'I shouldn't think you'll have the energy to stop up watching football after today,' she said.

Andrew grinned. Mum and Dad were always arguing about the telly. Things were getting back to normal.

What about his room? Andrew bounded up the stairs. Had Mum remembered how he liked things? She had. Snoopy was sitting on the pillow and his favourite poster hung on the wall. The rest didn't really matter, although he noticed there was a new cover on his bed, and a table-top thing under the window.

'Everything all right?' said Mum. 'Dad thought you might like a table so you can do your puzzles and things without losing bits up the vacuum.'

'Thank you,' said Andrew. Now even if they had a baby his Lego would be safe.

He must make sure though. If only to tell Joanne.

'Mum,' he said, as he crawled into bed. 'Are we going to have a baby?'

'Not to my knowledge,' Mum said, as she tucked him in. 'Whatever put that idea into your head?'

'Mrs Moore,' Andrew said.

Mother frowned.

'New house. New baby,' he explained.

'That's only a saying,' Mum laughed.

'Joanne's got a sister,' Andew said reprovingly. 'And a new house.'

'I know,' said Mum. 'But that was just the way it worked for them. Don't worry. You'd soon know if we were going to have a baby. There'd be so much to get ready. It's quite a thought though. Maybe you could talk to God about it in your prayers.'

Andrew snuggled under the new covers with Snoopy. There were so many things to talk to God about. The new house, Joanne, babies, school. But would God still be able to hear him now they'd moved house? Mum seemed to think so or she wouldn't have reminded him to say his prayers. What did his poster say? That was about God — the Jesus part of him.

He pulled himself up onto one elbow. The light from the hall shone in just the right place. It was easy to read.

'Jesus . . . the same yesterday, today, for ever.'

That was OK then. He should have remembered before. Whatever happened, God didn't change.

A blast of music blared from the television in the kitchen below.

Mum's voice shrilled in protest.

Andrew grinned. Neither did his parents by the sound of it.

The Helper

Joyce Frances Carpenter

'Oh dear!' whispered Jill under her breath. 'He's done it again!'

Opening her school desk, she pretended to find something and hid her blushes behind the open lid. When she and all the others in class were waiting to start morning lessons, Jill's twin brother was thudding along the corridor, late as usual! Some of the children had spotted Tom and were giggling. Tom was a regular joke to them — a sort of clown.

If Tom hurried he might just reach the classroom before the teacher arrived. Jill crossed her fingers hopefully. *Too late*. Mr Bates was now a few steps behind Tom. They arrived at the classroom door together and oh no! Tom had dropped all his exercise books and his box of pencils! A roar of laughter went up from the class. Tom's freckled face was scarlet and his ginger hair ruffled as he grovelled on the floor to pick them up.

Jill was fond of her twin, but when he made a fool of himself like this it made her see red. Mr Bates waited patiently for Tom to take his place in class. 'What's the excuse for being late this time, Tom?' he asked.

'My bike had a puncture,' Tom spluttered.

Jill remembered Tom had lagged behind on the three-mile ride to school. Tom's bike was often out of order. He didn't look after it.

Mr Bates returned the homework. 'Very good, Jill,' he smiled, handing back her sheet of neat writing. Next he held out a sheet covered in ink blots and crossings out. A smile went round the class. Everyone knew it was Tom's work.

Jill felt so cross with Tom for letting her down like this that she cycled home after school ahead of him and wouldn't speak to him all through tea.

It was Jill's turn that evening to help with the washing up. Mrs Ford washed while Jill dried. Tom had ambled off into the sitting-room. Jill didn't say a word. Her mum looked at Jill anxiously. 'What's the matter with you and Tom?' she asked.

'I'm fed up,' Jill exploded. 'Tom's always in trouble at school and it makes me look a fool when the other children laugh at him. He just doesn't *try* to improve.'

Her mum smiled. 'I'm sure Tom doesn't mean to do badly. He's naturally rather clumsy and forgetful you know.'

But Jill still felt cross about Tom. 'You just don't understand. It's awful for me at school. I want to have a brother I can be proud of,' she said grumpily.

She walked out of the kitchen and found Tom sprawled in a chair, eating sweets and watching his favourite sports programme on the telly. Something boiled up in Jill. Why should he look so happy and unconcerned? He had made her miserable at school. The way he was grinning at the telly annoyed her. She wanted revenge. She moved to the set and switched to the other channel.

'What did you do that for?' bawled Tom.

'I want the other station,' she yelled back.

'Jill, don't be mean. I was enjoying it.'

'Why should you always get your way?' Jill shouted.

Mum rushed into the room from the kitchen. 'Children. Stop quarrelling!' She hesitated and looked at Tom. 'Perhaps it is Jill's turn to see the programme she wants,' she said.

Jill sat back in triumph as she watched Tom walk slowly out of the room. Before long she could hear Tom bashing away at his football out in the garden. He must be furious about losing his precious sports programme — he was really murdering that ball. To be honest she wasn't really enjoying watching the telly. *Mean* — that's what Tom had called her. She was beginning to feel mean, becuse she had only switched over to spite him.

Crash! Jill and her mother jumped up from their seats as Tom's football shattered the glass in the sitting-room window.

'Tom! Come in and clear that up at once,' Mrs Ford shouted.

While Tom mumbled his apologies and swept the glass up his father arrived home. 'You'll pay for that, my lad. I'll stop it from your pocket-money,' he said firmly.

Poor Tom. Jill felt *awful* now. If she hadn't been spiteful and had let him watch his favourite programme this would never have happened. She felt miserable — it was horrible to think that being annoyed and a bit of bad temper could mount up to real trouble in no time at all!

Jill avoided Tom's eyes as he finished sweeping up the glass, and followed her mum into the kitchen. She watched her working carefully, mending the lining in her father's jacket with tiny neat stitches. She knew that Mum didn't really like sewing. Sometimes it made her cross.

'Poor Mum. That's a horrid job,' said Jill, sympathetically. 'Yes, it is,' answered Mum. 'But it's *my* job. My job is to help Dad — and it's his job to help me. Anyway, it's not really too bad. As long as I keep my temper,' she added, smiling.

Jill looked thoughtfully at her mum and in bed that night she considered the problem of Tom again. Couldn't she jog her brother's memory and help him a bit. Help him to help himself? Be a

helper like mum. Mum was a helper to all of them. When she said her prayers she asked God to help her to help Tom.

The next morning before breakfast Jill ran down to the garden shed and checked Tom's bike. His back tyre was flat. She pumped it up. It was the least she could do for having been so mean to him last night.

As they set off for school she blurted out, 'Tom, I'm sorry about the telly and the window and your pocket money and everything. It was all my fault.'

Tom grinned, 'That's okay. Forget it.' He was like that. Never bore a grudge.

Tom looked at his back tyre in amazement. 'Hey — did you pump it up for me?' he asked. She nodded. 'Thanks,' he muttered.

When they were half way to school Tom said suddenly, 'I know you get mad at me because I'm always late, Jill. Sorry about that.'

That morning was some kind of record because they were *both* early. The class looked at Tom in amazed surprise. What had happened? Jill gave a mischievous grin of triumph. Then she whispered to her brother, 'Keep it up, Tom!'

At that moment, they heard their teacher's footsteps in the corridor. Mr Bates was going to get the surprise of his life!

The King's Party

Geoff Treasure

Mr Stamp the postman looked at his sack and sighed. Sometimes his sack was almost empty. Today it was very full. Mr Stamp lifted his hat from his head and scratched his black hair.

'Wherever have all these letters come from?' he said to himself as he emptied the contents of the sack onto the floor.

Everywhere on the carpet were letters and parcels. There were small envelopes and large ones. Some were white, others were pink or blue. Today, though, Mr Stamp noticed that some of the envelopes were brown. He picked up one of them and looked at it carefully. He noticed four large letters in the corner of the envelope. O.H.M.S.

Mr Stamp repeated the four letters aloud. 'O.H.M.S. On . . . On His . . . On His Majesty's Service!' he exclaimed. 'This letter has come from the King himself!' He was so excited that he knelt down upon the floor and quickly searched through the pile of letters to see if there were any more brown envelopes with O.H.M.S. written upon them. There were. Mr Stamp put them into a pile and counted them carefully.

'One, two, three.'

A look of pride spread across his face.

'Fancy that!' he said. 'The King has written to three people in *our* small village. And those three letters are going into *my* sack!'

Mr Stamp felt very excited and very proud as he put his sack over his back, kissed his wife and set off to deliver his letters. All his letters were important but today he felt that three letters were even more important than the other ones which he was going to deliver. And if he felt proud and happy that morning, he was sure that the people to whom the King had written would feel even prouder and even happier.

There were many different kinds of houses in the village. And there were many different kinds of doors on the different kinds of houses. And behind those doors were many different kinds of people.

On the edge of the village was Honeysuckle Cottage. It was a very old house with a green, wooden door which creaked when it was opened. Honeysuckle grew all around the door. And behind the door lived Mr and Mrs Plough. Mr Plough was a farmer.

Mr Plough had been a farmer for many years. He wasn't a very rich man but he had many fields around his cottage. In some fields Mr Plough grew corn. In other fields Mr Plough's sheep were grazing.

Mr Stamp opened the gate and walked up the path. He looked again at the brown envelope with the four letters in the corner. He dropped it through the letter-box just as Mr Plough was coming back from the fields for his breakfast.

Mr Stamp looked at the second brown envelope. Although he did not know the person to whom it was written, he knew the road where he lived. He often delivered letters there.

Success Lodge was the biggest house in the road. It had been built at the top of the hill some years before. It had a large garden surrounded by a high wall. The only way into the garden was through two large iron gates. Mr Stamp looked at the name upon the gates and then at the address upon the brown envelope. So the King had also written to Mr Shares, the owner of Success Lodge.

Mr Stamp walked up the long path to the front door. The gravel crunched beneath his feet. He knew the path well. Mr Shares had letters every day.

Mr Shares did not work in the village. Every morning he kissed his wife goodbye and drove into town in his big, shiny car. He worked in an office in a tall building. His job was to buy and sell land. People in the village said that he was a very rich man. Mr Stamp had often wondered what it was like behind the thick, red door of Success Lodge.

He took the brown envelope from his pile of letters and pushed it through the brass letter-box. As Mr Stamp walked down the drive, Mr Shares was just coming to the front door. He picked up the brown envelope and put it into his case. He waved to his wife, got into his car and drove off to work.

By now Mr Stamp's sack was much lighter. Most of his letters and small parcels had been delivered. But still there was one brown envelope with four letters in the corner. Mr Stamp looked again at the address and smiled.

'Mr Newly-Wed, Cranstone Close,' he said aloud to himself.

He knew this part of the village well. All the houses were new. They were built close together and it didn't take long to deliver letters to the people who lived there. Mr and Mrs Newly-Wed lived at Number Three Cranstone Close. As Mr Stamp pushed the King's letter through the letter-box, Mr Newly-Wed was just getting up.

Later that day Mr Plough, Mr Shares and Mr Newly-Wed all read the letter that they had received from the King. Each letter said the same thing:

'You are invited to a party
to be held at the Palace
on Thursday next at 8.00 p.m.
Please reply to the King.'

'A letter to me from the King!' exclaimed a surprised Mr Plough.

'Another invitation to a party,' said a bored Mr Shares.

'The King wants me to attend his party,' said Mr Newly-Wed.

'You had better reply straightaway,' said Mrs Plough.

'Take a letter, Miss Jones,' said Mr Shares to his secretary.

'I have bought a card for you to send in reply to the King's invitation,' said Mrs Newly-Wed.

And so three letters were written to the King, placed in the post-box in the middle of the village and later delivered to the Royal Palace.

The King was very excited when his servant brought in the post that day. He had spent a lot of money preparing for the party. He had chosen the largest room in the palace. His cooks were preparing the finest food that money could buy. His musicians were practising music to play to all the guests. The King was looking forward to his party and he was sure that all those who had been invited would be looking forward to the party, too.

So the King picked up the first envelope and opened it. He read Mr Plough's reply.

'Your Majesty,
Thank you for your invitation to the party. I am sorry but I cannot come. I have just bought a new tractor. I want to go into the field and try it out.
Mr Plough, the Farmer.'

The King was most surprised. He picked up the second envelope, opened it and pulled out the letter from Mr Shares.

'Your Majesty,
Thank you for your invitation to the party. I am sorry but I cannot come. I have to go and look at some land which I have bought.
Mr Shares.'

The King was most surprised and annoyed. Two invitations to his party and both of them rejected. 'Surely,' he thought as he picked up another envelope, 'surely there must be some people who want to come to my party.'
He pulled the letter from the envelope and read it slowly. It was from Mr Newly-Wed.

'Your Majesty,
Thank you for your invitation to the

party. I am sorry but I cannot come. I have just got married and I want to introduce my new wife to some friends.

Mr Newly-Wed.'

The King was most surprised, annoyed and very, very, angry. His face grew red, his nose twitched and his mouth opened wide.

'Who would believe it!' he exclaimed. 'Nobody wants to come to my party. I have spent pounds and pounds preparing for this party and Mr Plough thinks that a tractor is more important than I am!'

All the servants nodded understandingly as the king spoke. 'I have asked my cooks to prepare the very best food that money can buy and yet Mr Shares thinks that a piece of land is more important than I am!'

The servants nodded again. They couldn't understand why Mr Plough or Mr Shares had refused to come to the party. 'I have gathered together the finest musicians in the land to play the loveliest music and Mr Newly-Wed thinks that an evening with friends and his new wife is more important than an evening with me in my Palace.'

The King strode up and down his room. His servants looked at him, wondering what he would do next. It seemed such a pity to waste the food, the music and all the money which the king had spent. Surely there were some people somewhere who would like to come to the King's party!

The King called his servants to him.

'Mr Plough, Mr Shares and Mr Newly-Wed have refused to come to my party,' he said. 'Now I want you to go out into the village and to invite everyone you see to come to my party.'

The servants looked surprised.

'Everyone?' they asked.

'Everyone,' answered the King.

The servants were amazed. They couldn't believe it.

'Yes, everyone,' said the King again. 'That means everyone who is out of work. It means beggars and poor men. People who are not wanted, not loved, not cared for, people who have no friends or only a few friends, people dressed in rags, people who are dirty, who are sick, people who have no home. Tell them all that the King wants them to come to his party!'

Off the servants ran. Down the drive from the palace door, into the road which passed outside, on and on they ran. Along wide roads and down narrow lanes they ran — quickly and hurriedly down the hills, slowly and panting up the hills. And whenever they saw anyone, they shouted, 'The King wants you to come to his party!'

'Me?' said the poor man.

'You,' said the servant.

'Me?' said the ragged man, pulling his rags around him.

'You,' said the servant.

'Me?' said the sick man, lying by himself under a tree.

'Yes, you,' said the servant. 'The King wants you to come to his party.

'And you
    and you
        and you
            and you!
Everyone is invited to the King's party.'

Soon the road to the palace was filled with people. In fact there were so many people going to the party at the palace that Mr Plough found it difficult to get to his tractor; Mr Shares was late getting to see the land which he had bought and Mr and Mrs Newly-Wed missed their bus to visit their friends. At the end of the day they were quite miserable. But all those who came to the King's party were very happy that night. They were glad that they had said 'yes' to the King.

Ally Gives
a Christmas Present

Thelma Sangster

There was a tingling feeling of excitement in the air at 33 Beckett Street. Christmas was coming.

Ally and Mum stirred the Christmas pudding. It smelt sweet and spicy. Andy stood by, ready to lick spoons.

Mum opened the kitchen cupboard. She brought down six little silver things from a high shelf. She washed them well and popped them into the pudding mix for the family to 'find' at Christmas dinner.

Ally's eyes sparkled as Mum stirred them in — wishbone, cradle, train, button, dog and sledge. She hoped she would find the cradle. Andy wanted the train.

There was a sound of hammering coming from the garden shed. Dad was making something — but they weren't allowed to see it.

'It's a doll's house,' Ally confided to Belinda May as she put the baby doll to sleep in her cradle. She tucked her in with the pretty patchwork quilt

Mum had made. It was special — Mum had made it from little bits of material left over from making dresses for Ally.

'It's a car! Vroom . . . vroom,' shouted Andy, running into the room and out again.

Christmas was coming at play-group too. Miss Carter had taught the children to sing carols. They had decorated the hall with tinsel and streamers and stuck cotton wool on the windows and made a snowman out of white tissue paper scraps stuck on a cone of newspaper.

'Everyone will have a part in the Christmas play,' Miss Carter had told them. First she chose the youngest children to be lambs. They wore woolly face-masks and tails, and crawled in, making bleating sounds.

Then Miss Carter picked Lindy to be Mary, and gave her a baby doll to hold. Ally frowned. Lindy always got the nice parts.

Gary was to be Joseph. He had to lead Mary in and say, 'Inn-keeper, my wife is tired. Have you any room in the inn?'

And Sandra (who giggled a lot) had to answer, 'No, there is no room in the inn, but there is room in the stable. Follow me.'

'Ally, you can be a shepherd,' Miss Carter said, handing her a striped curtain for her costume. Ally made a face. She wanted to be Mary, and hold the baby Jesus.

Andy could speak up in a nice loud voice, so Miss Carter made him the Angel. But Andy was against the idea.

'Want to be a racing-driver,' he announced. And he vroom-vroomed to the end of the hall.

Miss Carter fetched him back. 'Well, we can't have a racing-driver in this play. You'll have to be an Angel,' she said in a voice that meant, 'It's fixed'.

But somehow rehearsals had not gone at all smoothly.

Ally had to point to the Angel and say, 'What's that light?' But she was never ready, and had to be poked.

The Angel was supposed to say, 'Behold I bring good news. A Saviour is born today' . . . but he kept forgetting his words.

And when Gary said to Sandra 'Idd-keeper, by wife is tired. Have you eddy roob?' (because he had a cold), Sandra had a fit of the giggles and spoilt her lines.

But Miss Carter was very patient. 'It will be all right on the day when your parents come,' she said.

So today Mum was making the Angel a long white robe out of an old sheet. Andy tried it on. When he lifted his arms the wings spread out.

'Vroom-vroom,' shouted Andy, jumping off the sofa. He tripped on the hem and made a crash landing. His yells brought everyone running.

Dad picked him up. 'Come and see what I've been making,' he said.

They all went out to the shed. It was growing dark in the garden, but the first star of the evening hung in the clear, frosty sky. It winked at Ally.

In the bare wooden hut Dad had hung up a storm lantern. Its light shone on a group of small figures, grouped on the work-bench. They were carved from wood, with painted faces and bodies. Three had gold crowns on their heads. There were shepherds and some animals too.

Ally could see Mary dressed in blue by the manger, with Joseph standing beside her. The little baby in the crib looked like a real baby, asleep. She thought he looked cold.

'Ooh . . . lovely,' said Ally. 'Can we keep it?'

'No, I've made it for the shop window display to remind people what Christmas is all about,' said Daddy. 'It's to remind them that the reason we give presents is because God gave his Son for us.'

Ally glanced round the bare cold shed. She looked at Dad's tools all neatly laid out. She smelt the wood shavings, swept into a neat pile. Her guinea-pigs Spick and Span squeaked softly from their winter quarters on a nearby shelf.

Ally turned and ran from the shed, up to her bedroom. Snatching up little Belinda May's soft, warm quilt of patchwork squares she said to the

little doll, 'Jesus needs it, Belinda May'. She put the doll into her own bed and Belinda's eyes closed trustingly in sleep.

Out in the shed Ally placed the patchwork quilt over the little figure in the cradle. 'A present for baby Jesus,' she said.

Mum put an arm around her. Ally glimpsed the star, winking in the cold night, through the shed window. She suddenly felt all right about being a shepherd in the Christmas play.

Going over to the guinea-pigs she took Spick and Span from their nesting-boxes. Then she bent over the cradle, holding one under each arm. 'Look — sheep,' she said.

Suddenly the Angel spoke up loud and clear: 'Behold I bring you good news. A Saviour is born today . . .' And he lifted his arms to let the wings show.

And Ally knew everything was going to be all right.

The Day the Fair Came

Margaret Ralph

'Hurry up, Cathie. Breakfast's ready.'

Her mum stood at the kitchen door and called for the third time.

'Shut up,' muttered Cathie under her breath. She turned over and pulled the bedclothes further up round her ears.

'Why should I get up?' she thought. Just because the boys have got another day at school and Dad has to go to work. I've started my summer holidays.

'Catherine,' called her mother sternly.

Cathie knew then that she must get up. When Mum used her full name like that she meant what she said.

Slowly she pushed back the bedclothes and rolled out of bed. Once out she forgot to be cross. For she suddenly remembered something exciting. Today was the day the fair was coming. Karen and Sally had promised to take her.

She dressed quickly and hurried out to the kitchen, smoothing her hair as she went. The rest of the family were already sitting round the table.

'Here comes Cathie, slow as a snail,
Always behind like the cow's tail,'

chanted Kevin, waving his spoon in the air.

'I'm not . . .' began Cathie hotly, but her mum interrupted.

'Sit down and get on with your breakfast, love.' She poured some milk on to Cathie's cereal. 'We're not on holiday yet you know.'

Cathie sat down and did as she was told. She did not speak again until she had finished her cereal. Then she looked up at her mum.

'The fair's coming today,' she said.

'Is it,' answered her mum, not really listening.

'They were putting the things up last night in the Rec,' went on Cathie. 'Can I go?'

Her mum turned to look at her. 'No, I don't think so, love, not on your own.'

'Not on my own,' said Cathie. 'With Karen and Sally.'

Her mum looked doubtful. 'They are not very old,' she said, 'to go into all that crowd.'

'Oh, Mum,' pouted Cathie. 'They are two years older than me and you always say I'm all right with them.'

'I know,' admitted her mum, 'but not at the fair.'

Cathie's dad joined in. 'You need money for fairs,' he said. 'Where is the money coming from?'

'I've got plenty in my money-box,' said Cathie.

Her dad laughed. 'Don't forget we are going on holiday next week. You'll need all your pocket money then. I can't afford to give you any more.'

Cathie was silent, thinking. That's just what Karen and Sally had said. 'You can come with us if you've got some money,' they had said, last night. 'You need money for fairs.' Cathie remembered how they had looked at one another as they spoke.

Presently she tried again. 'I wouldn't spend much of my money, Mum,' she pleaded. 'Only about 20p. And I wouldn't stay long.'

Her mother was rushing the boys off to school. 'No, Cathie,' she snapped. 'You heard what your dad said. You can't go, and that's that.'

Cathie sighed and said no more, but she went on thinking about it. 'I wonder how much there is in my money-box?' she said to herself. 'I think I'll just count it and see.'

When her mum was busy in the kitchen she went into her bedroom and shut the door. Carefully she lifted her money-box down from the shelf. It was a fat china pig with Clacton written across its back. Her dad had bought it for her when they were on holiday last year. Quickly she shook the money out on to the bed. There was a pound note which her gran had given her the last time she visited them. She counted the coins — two fives, eight tens and seven pennies.

'Look at that,' she said aloud. 'There's plenty there. Why shouldn't I go to the fair?'

Slowly she made up her mind. 'I'll leave the pound note for next week and just take the coins,' she said. 'I don't care what Mum says.'

She took out her purse and began to put in the tens.

'Perhaps I'll just put the pound note in in case I need it,' she thought, 'but I won't spend it.' She folded it and slipped it into the inside pocket, then zipped up the purse and shook it to hear the coins clinking together.

She hid the purse under her pillow and smoothed the bedspread. Then she left her bedroom and went out of the flat door on to the landing. Leaning over the rails she could see right down into the entrance hall five floors below. All was quiet except for the clink of bottles and the cheery whistle of the milkman as he made his way up.

She heard slow footsteps and heavy breathing. That was old Mrs Barrett from next door. The lift must be out of order again. Cathie ran down the stairs to help her carry her bag of groceries. Mrs Barrett always gave her a biscuit when she did this. Today it was a ginger nut. She went out on to the landing again, munching.

On the floor above a door banged and a woman's voice shouted crossly. It was Karen's mum. There was the patter of two pairs of feet running downstairs and Karen and Sally appeared.

'Will your mum let you come to the fair?' asked Sally, seeing Cathie.

Cathie ignored the first part of the question. 'Yes, I'm coming,' she said.

'Don't forget your money then,' called Karen as they passed on down the stairs. 'We shall be leaving at two.'

Cathie went in to wait for dinner time.

'When are we having dinner, Mum?' she asked at half past twelve. 'I'm hungry.'

'Not just yet, love,' answered her mother. 'I've got to get this ironing finished first. There's only one more day before the holiday, and you will all need plenty of clean clothes then.'

Cathie tried to wait patiently.

At last her mother switched off the iron and folded up the ironing board.

'Scrambled egg all right?' she asked Cathie. 'There isn't time to cook much now.'

'Can't we have some of those sausages?' asked Cathie, peering round the back of her mum into the fridge.

'No,' said her mum, shutting the fridge door firmly. 'They are for tomorrow when the boys are home.'

Cathie sighed. 'All right then. Scrambled egg,' she agreed. She loved sausages, especially with beans.

'Come and help me dry up,' said her mother after dinner. Unwillingly Cathie went, not daring to make a fuss. She dried the knives and forks in record time, longing to get out on to the landing before Karen and Sally knocked at the door.

At last she finished and went into the living-room. Her mother was still in the kitchen. Cathie tiptoed into her bedroom, pulled out her purse from its hiding place and let herself out of the flat door, shutting it quietly behind her. As she did so Karen and Sally came running down the stairs.

'Have you brought your money?' Sally asked, as soon as they were out of the building.

Cathie held out her purse and Sally took it from her. She unzipped it and looked inside, smiling as she held it out for Karen to see.

'I'd better look after this for you,' she said. 'It would be awful if you lost it.'

Cathie did not mind. She felt proud to be out with the older girls. It was not far to the Rec.

'What shall we do first?' asked Sally as they went in.

'Let Cathie choose,' said Karen kindly.

Cathie looked round, bewildered. The Rec was full of noise and movement. Roundabouts sped swiftly on their tracks. Harsh music blared forth. From the stalls men shouted. There were people everywhere, children and grown-ups, watching.

'Let's have a look round first,' said Cathie. So they did.

There were roundabouts of all kinds. One had helicopters and aeroplanes, one space-ships, and another cars, fire-engines and lifeboats.

Then Cathie saw it, the real roundabout with horses. That was what her gran had told her about when she came to stay. It was what had made Cathie long to go to the fair. She stood for a long time watching it with shining eyes.

'I'd love to go on that,' she said at last, turning to Sally and Karen.

'OK. Let's go,' said Sally.

She paid the man for three tickets and they chose their horses. The horses were in pairs.

'Do you want to ride on your own or with one of us?' asked Karen.

'I'd like to ride with you,' replied Cathie.

'Come on then,' said Karen, and climbed on to the front seat.

Cathie climbed up behind her and settled in to the saddle. Sally clambered on to the horse beside them.

The roundabout began to move, slowly at first. Cathie clung on to the twisty pole which joined the horse to the roundabout. Gradually they gained speed, swinging gently up and down as they went. Cathie closed her eyes and revelled in the smooth motion. She relaxed a little and patted her horse's side gently, whispering 'Go on, boy, go on, good boy.'

Too soon, they began to slow down and come to a standstill. Cathie climbed off and went to the horse's head to say goodbye.

'Next time I'll ride in front,' she said, 'then I can really talk to you properly.'

'Shall we have some candy floss?' asked Sally.

'Yes,' agreed Cathie, who had never tasted it.

The mass of pink fluff looked enormous but Cathie found that as soon as her lips touched it, it seemed to disappear leaving a sweet sticky taste in her mouth. 'Funny stuff,' she said, and felt a bit disappointed.

They stood watching the big wheel. It was so high that Cathie had to tilt her head back to see the top of it. She shivered a little as she watched.

'Going on?' Sally asked Karen.

Karen looked doubtful. 'What about Cathie?' she asked.

'She'll have to wait,' said Sally. 'She's only a kid. She won't go on. She wouldn't dare.'

She looked scornfully at Cathie as she spoke and Cathie flushed. She was afraid but she hated to be called a kid. Perhaps it wasn't as bad as it looked.

'I'll go,' she said, trying to sound as if she really wanted to.

'No, Cathie —' began Karen, but Sally interrupted.

'Shut up, Karen. let her go if she wants to. You are worse than she is.'

So they all went. It wasn't as bad as it looked. It didn't move so very fast and there was a bar fastened in front to stop you from falling out. The worst part was when they got right to the top and began moving down again. For a moment Cathie thought she was going to crash down into the crowd of people looking up. She closed her eyes quickly and when she looked again they were at the bottom. She was glad to get off.

Shrieks and yells were coming from one corner of the field so they went to see what was happening. They saw an enormous roundabout with seats which were swinging about and lurching in all directions as they moved. It made Cathie feel giddy to look at it.

'Coming on this one?' asked Sally, looking at Karen.

'OK.' said Karen. 'What about you, Cathie?'

Cathie knew when she had had enough. She shook her head. 'I'll wait for you here,' she said.

At first the two girls laughed and waved as they passed her. But soon they were clinging on and their faces were grim. Round and round they swung. Backwards and forwards lurched the seats. It seemed a long time before they slowed down and Karen and Sally staggered off. Sally's face was green.

'You all right, Sally?' asked Karen.

'Course I'm all right,' snapped Sally, turning her back on them.

She went and leaned over a bar, watching some men throwing darts. Karen and Cathie followed and they all watched silently. They wandered round all the stalls then, looking at coconut shies and rifle shooting.

They bought some popcorn and an ice lolly.

They tried catching coloured balls in a fishing net but they didn't win anything.

'You've got enough money left for one more ride,' said Sally at last. 'What do you want to go on?'

'The bumping cars,' replied Cathie at once.

'OK then.' For the last time Sally bought three tickets.

It was great being on the bumper cars. Cathie really felt she was driving as she whizzed round the course, gripping the steering-wheel tightly. 'This is the best thing of all,' she thought happily.

All too soon it was over. Sally and Karen got off quickly.

'You might as well have your purse now,' called Sally, tossing it to her in the car.

Cathie searched on the floor to find it and when she stood up Karen and Sally had disappeared. She jumped hastily from the car and her dress caught on the seat. There was a sharp sound of tearing cloth as she jumped. Cathie groaned and looked down to see a long tear in her skirt.

'Mum will be furious, especially just before we go on holiday,' she thought.

She wandered about looking for Karen and Sally but they were nowhere to be seen. Then the smell of chips from a nearby stall reminded her that she was hungry. She brightened. 'I've still got my pound,' she said to herself. 'I'll buy a bag of chips before I go home.'

She opened her purse and felt in the inside pocket. The pound note was not there. She opened the purse wide and peered inside. It was quite empty.

'Sally must have spent all my money,' she said aloud.

For the first time she realized the trouble she was in. She had come to the fair without her mum knowing, her dress was torn and all her money was gone. How could she possibly go home?

She wandered miserably round the fairground, trying to think of a way out of her troubles. She did not notice where she was going until she looked up to find herself among a group of caravans.

On the step of one of them sat a boy, reading a comic. He looked up as Cathie came near.

'What're you doing here?' he called. 'This is private.'

Cathie stood silent, looking about her uncertainly.

'You lost?' asked the boy.

Cathie shook her head. 'No-o,' she replied doubtfully, 'not lost, but I can't go home.'

'Why not?' He looked curious.

Cathie was tired and glad of someone to talk to. She sat down on the step and told him all about it.

'So I just can't go home,' she finished, 'with no money and a torn dress.'

The boy laughed. 'Sounds like the story on the back of my comic,' he remarked.

'What's that?' asked Cathie, looking over.

'It's about a boy who ran away from home and spent all his money,' said the boy. 'Look, he was in rags and hadn't even enough to eat. Then he remembered his dad and decided to go home. As soon as his dad saw him coming he ran out to meet him and gave him new clothes and made a special supper for him.'

'My dad isn't like that,' sighed Cathie. 'That's a made-up story.'

'It's not made-up. It's out of the Bible,' explained the boy. 'I think the father's meant to be God.'

Cathie frowned. 'What's God got to do with running away?' she asked.

'Dunno, except it says God's our father and when we do something wrong it's like running away from God,' he said. 'But if we are sorry he always takes us back, like the one in the story.'

'Oh!' Cathie was thinking about her own father. 'My dad loves me but I reckon he'll be awful mad at me this time,' she said.

'I should take a chance on it,' said the boy.

Cathie didn't answer. She was thinking of them all at home now. The boys would be back from school and Dad would have come home from work. Were they wondering where she was? They would be having tea. The more she thought of them the more she longed to be there. Even if they are cross it will be worth it, she thought. I know I shouldn't have done it, it was stupid of me, and I'll tell them I'm sorry.

'I think I'll go home now,' she said at last, standing up.

'Good luck,' replied the boy.

Cathie walked away and saw a tall policeman coming towards her.

'What are you doing, all on your own, at this time of day?' he asked, stopping in front of her.

'I've been to the fair and I-I'm just going home,' stammered Cathie.

The policeman bent down and spoke gently. 'What's your name, love?'

'Cathie,' she said, 'Catherine Starwell.'

'I'll say you are going home,' he said. 'At once, and with me.' He straightened up and took her by the hand.

'Do you know your mum and dad are just about doing their nut over you?' he asked.

Cathie shook her head. 'Are they very cross?' she whispered.

'They are worried stiff,' he replied. 'And if they are cross you deserve it.'

'I know,' admitted Cathie, meekly.

When they reached his car he opened the door wide. 'Hop in,' he said, and got into the driving seat.

First he radioed the police station. Then he drove her swiftly home through the darkening streets.

As the police car drew up in front of the flats the big swing doors burst open and her mum came running out.

'Oh, there you are, Cathie,' she cried. 'Wherever have you been?'

'I found her at the fair,' said the policeman. 'She told me she was just coming home.'

At that moment Cathie's dad came hurrying along the road.

'They told me at the police station she was on the way home,' he explained, looking around at them. 'Is she all right?'

'Right as rain,' replied the policeman. 'So all's well that ends well. But don't you let it happen again, young lady. You stay at home until your dad can take you to the fair.'

'Thank you for finding her,' said Cathie's dad.

'Glad to have been of service,' answered the policeman, smiling, and went back to to his car.

Together they went into the flats and up in the mended lift.

'Why did you do it, Cathie?' asked her mum, as they stood facing one another. 'We were worried sick about you. We thought you might be dead.'

'Never mind that now,' said her dad, putting his arms round them both. 'She's safe and that's all that really matters. We'll talk about the rest later.'

The lift stopped and they got out. As they opened the flat door the boys came running out of the kitchen.

'We've watched the sausages, Mum, and they're cooking fine,' said Kevin.

'As soon as I knew you were on the way home I put on some sausages and beans,' said her mum, looking at Cathie. 'I know you like them and I thought we'd have a treat.'

'Not that you deserve any treats,' said her dad, but his arm was round her and his voice was not cross.

Cathie felt a warm feeling inside her. Her mind went back to the boy on the caravan step, reading his comic.

'If God is like that I wish I could get to know him,' she thought.

Under the Golden Throne
By Ralph Batten

'Under the golden throne, in the palace of the High King, lay Shamar, the one and only dog of Patria. Slowly he yawned and opened a big, brown eye . . .'

In the seven tales of Shamar the dog, we meet a wealth of comic characters, including the self-important Prime Minister of Patria, the fussy Chancellor of the Exchequer and the dignified Derel the Wise. And, of course, the delightfully stupid Seven Knights of the Realm.

Each story tells of an adventure of Shamar the dog and his beloved master, the High King of Patria. And at the end of each story, Shamar settles down under the golden throne and sleeps. And as he sleeps, he dreams a dream . . .

The Haffertee Hamster Series

by Janet and John Perkins

'Even though I say it myself, I'm quite a character.'
Haffertee is a lovable, lively soft-toy hamster
whose funny adventures help children think about
the world around them, about their relationships
and about God. Each charmingly-illustrated book
contains ten short stories, ideal for reading aloud.

The Incredible Will of H. R. Heartman
by Jean Harmeling

Timothy Heartman is running away — away from the children's home, away from the fussy Miss Farfyle and the evil Mr. Biggs.

For Timothy, an orphan, is about to gain a fortune. One of the richest men in the world has left him everything — on the condition that Timothy takes twelve special pictures with the camera provided. A crumpled piece of parchment with a mysterious message is all he has to help him. . .

This zany adventure story is full of excitement, humour and suspense.